Paddington

at the Zoo

Michael Bond

Paddington

at the Zoo

illustrated by R.W. ALLEY

HarperCollins *Children's Books*

One day Jonathan and Judy decided to take Paddington on an outing to the zoo.

Before they set off Paddington made a large pile of marmalade sandwiches – six in all.

But when they reached the zoo, the gatekeeper wouldn't let them in.

"I'm sorry," he said. "Pets aren't allowed."

"Pets!" repeated Jonathan.

"Paddington isn't a *pet*," said Judy. "He's one of the family."

And Paddington gave the man such a hard stare he let them in without another word.

"Come on," said Jonathan. "Why don't I take your picture with the parrot?"

"Give a great big smile," called Judy. "Say cheese!"

"Cheese," said Paddington.

"Squawk!" said a parrot as it took a big bite out of Paddington's sandwich. "Thank you very much. Squawk! Squawk!"

Next they went to see the Siberian Wild Dog.

"Nice doggie," said Paddington.

But the Siberian Wild Dog went,
"Owwowwwowwwoo!" and made Paddington
jump so much the rest of the sandwich flew out
of his hand and landed
in the cage.

"Let me take a picture of you with a donkey,"
said Jonathan.

"Hee! Haw!" brayed the donkey when it saw
Paddington's sandwiches.

"That's two gone," said Judy.

Paddington's smile was getting less cheesy all
the time.

The elephant didn't wait to be asked either. It simply made a loud trumpeting noise — "Whoooohoowooo!" — and reached down with its trunk.

Paddington watched as his third sandwich
disappeared. He began to feel that going to the
zoo was not such a good idea after all.

But there was worse to follow.

When the lion saw them coming, it gave a
great roar – "Grrrrrrrrrahh!"

It was such a loud roar Paddington dropped his
fourth sandwich on the ground and before he
could say "help" it was surrounded by pigeons.

The only ones who didn't
say anything were the
penguins. They just stood
there looking sad, as if
they were all dressed up
for a party but had
nowhere to go.

Paddington felt so sorry
for them he gave them
sandwich number five.

"Penguins eat fish,"
said a man sternly. He
pointed to a notice. "It is
strictly forbidden to give
them marmalade
sandwiches."

And while Paddington was looking at the notice,
the man helped himself to the last
of the sandwiches!

"The cheek of it!" said Jonathan.

"You need eyes in the back of your head,"
agreed Judy.

"I need my elevenses," said Paddington.
"Zoos make you hungry. Besides, nothing more
can happen to me now."

But it did. Just to round things off, the
mountain goat ate his sandwich bag!

"That does it!" said Jonathan. "If you ask me,
it's time we went home."

A few days later Jonathan showed Paddington the photographs he'd taken at the zoo. "You can have one for your scrap book," he said.

"Which do you like best?"
asked Judy.

"The one with the parrot," said Paddington promptly. "At least he said 'thank you' when he ate my marmalade sandwich. That's more than any of the others did!"

First published in hardback in Great Britain by HarperCollins*Publishers* in 1984
First published in paperback by Collins Picture Books in 2000
Published as part of a gift set by HarperCollins Children's Books in 2007

5 7 9 10 8 6 4

Collins Picture Books is an imprint of the Children's Division, part of HarperCollins Publishers Ltd.
HarperCollins Children's Books is a division of HarperCollins Publishers Ltd.

Text copyright © Michael Bond 1984
Illustrations copyright © R.W. Alley 1998

Visit our website at: www.harpercollins.co.uk

Printed and bound in China